Bloomsbury Education
An imprint of Bloomsbury Publishing Plc

50 Bedford Square
London
WC1B 3DP
UK

1385 Broadway
New York
NY 10018
USA

www.bloomsbury.com

MIX
Paper
FSC FSC® C020056

This book is produced using paper that is made from wood grown in managed, sustainable forests. It is natural, renewable and recyclable. The logging and manufacturing processes conform to the environmental regulations of the country of origin.

To find out more about our authors and books visit www.bloomsbury.com. Here you will find extracts, author interviews, details of forthcoming events and the option to sign up for our newsletters.

recommended by

www.catchup.org

Catch Up is a charity which aims to address the problem of underachievement that has its roots in literacy and numeracy difficulties

JUDY WAITE

CHELSEA'S STORY

Illustrated by Chris Askham

BLOOMSBURY EDUCATION
AN IMPRINT OF BLOOMSBURY

LONDON OXFORD NEW YORK NEW DELHI SYDNEY

THE STREET

Lena, Kai, Sanjay and Chelsea live on Swatton High Street.

They are fourteen years old, and they are best friends. They'll never let each other down...

CONTENTS

Chapter One
The Chase

Chelsea walked fast. Fast enough to get away from the gang of girls who were following her. She was trying not to run. Running would make her look like a wimp.

"You sc-sc-sc-scared?" one of them called.

"Hey Whitney, did you see her face when she saw us in the park?" a second voice asked. "She looked like a rabbit in headlights."

Chelsea realised it had been a bad choice to head away from the park and down the alley. She could get trapped. Chelsea had never been in a fight. The gang would probably pull her hair. They would scratch and kick.

She broke into a jog.

"Run, rabbit, run," sang the girls.

Chelsea didn't think they would bother to run after her.

They were the skinny-jean, high-heeled type and running wouldn't be cool.

Behind her, she heard more laughter. "Let her go," the girl called Whitney said. "Poor little rabbit."

Chelsea jogged on to the end of the alley, then raced across the street to her home in The Crown pub. Mum was watering the flower tubs outside.

"You look hot," Mum said. "Your face is pinker than these roses."

Chelsea didn't want to tell Mum she'd just been scared by a gang of girls. Mum might make things worse by trying to get involved.

"Hi. You OK?" called a voice from across the street. It was Kai, one of Chelsea's best friends.

"Hi. Yeah, great." Chelsea didn't want Kai to know she'd been scared either. She wanted to keep the whole thing a secret.

Mum turned to smile at Kai. "Maybe you could help Chelsea out?" she called.

Kai came to join them. "With what?" Kai asked.

"She could do with something to keep her occupied, rather than just hanging about with you, Lena and Sanjay like she did last summer holidays," said Chelsea's mum.

"Muuum!" Chelsea could feel her face blushing pinker than ever. It was as if she was invisible. And anyway, what was wrong with spending the holidays with her three best friends?

Kai laughed. "You think we just hang about?" he said. "I've signed up for a kickboxing tournament. I'm training all summer. The gym got broken into a while back but everything's new now. It's awesome."

"Take Chelsea to the gym with you," said Mum. "She could learn kickboxing, too."

"Mum!" Chelsea said. She was sure she would be rubbish at kickboxing.

Kai put his arm round Chelsea. "OK. There's a new class starting tomorrow. It's for beginners and it's on twice a week."

Chelsea felt goose bumps when Kai touched her. Kai was a friend; she really liked him... in fact she more than liked him. She kept it a secret though. Even her best friend Lena didn't know. "That's decided then," said Mum. She turned back to the flowers. "Kickboxing will impress Tommy, too. He is coming home in two weeks."

Chelsea glowed at the thought. Her brother Tommy was away in the army and she missed him.

Her dad had left when she was five. Since then, Tommy had taken his place. He always looked out for her.

Three girls walked past. They were from the gang and they strutted like supermodels. The tallest one narrowed her eyes at Chelsea, as if she was going to say something, but then she just laughed and walked on.

"What were you laughing at, Whitney?" one of the other girls asked.

"Nothing," said Whitney. "Or at least, nothing important."

Chelsea watched them walk away. She knew why Whitney had said 'nothing important'.

What Whitney was really saying was that **she** wasn't important. She was someone who didn't matter at all.

Chelsea knew she had to learn to deal with girls like Whitney. Kickboxing might really help her feel braver. Perhaps she should give it a try. One of Tommy's favourite sayings was 'Don't go, never know.'

"OK," she shrugged. "I'll sign up for kickboxing."

She hoped she wouldn't make a major idiot of herself.

Chapter Two
Spitting Tiger

Chelsea looked around the gym. It was mostly young guys punching bags. Two girls were fighting in a ring with ropes around it. Everyone wore kit with the Spitting Tiger logo on it.

Chelsea had come in leggings and a T-shirt. "I feel like a geek," she said.

"You'll fit in fine. This is a great club," said Kai.

Chelsea frowned. "Those helmets and gloves and knee-pad things... are they here because you can get badly hurt?" she asked.

"Only if you don't know what you're doing," said Kai. He must have noticed how worried Chelsea looked. "It's mostly non-contact," he added.

"What does non-contact mean?" asked Chelsea.

"It means your opponents will only pretend to punch you on the nose," laughed Kai.

A man stepped out from an office doorway.

"How's it going, Kai? You brought your girlfriend to cheer you on?" he asked.

Kai grinned. "Nah, Darren, she's not my girlfriend – just my girl **friend**."

"Good plan. Look where romance got me. Married. Divorced. We both lost money when we sold the house, and now I'm back to renting a flat again. It's hardly living the dream," said Darren.

Chelsea snuck a look at Darren. He seemed tough. Chelsea imagined him watching her trying to kickbox, while she lurched about like a goofy giraffe.

"Chelsea's just signed up for the beginners' class," said Kai.

"Liz is running that one. It's in the basement. Starts in ten minutes." Darren turned back to Kai. "It's impressive that you've made it to first Dan black belt. First Dan is a high level for someone your age. You'll do well at the tournament," Darren added.

"Awesome." Darren's compliments made Kai glow. Chelsea could see how happy he was.

Someone touched her shoulder. "Are you here for beginners?" a voice asked.

Chelsea turned to see a slim, dark-haired woman with a ponytail. The Spitting Tiger kit really suited her.

"Um – yeah – my name's Chelsea."

"I'm Liz. Don't look so worried." Liz took Chelsea's arm and steered her away from Kai and Darren. "There won't be anything difficult," Liz said. "It'll be fun."

Chelsea glanced round to wave goodbye to Kai, but he was walking towards the ring with Darren.

It looked as if he had already forgotten about her.

Chapter Three
The Invisible Girl

"You seriously taking up kickboxing? With Kai?" Lena said.

Lena and Chelsea lay on towels in Lena's back garden, working on their tans. Or at least, Lena was obsessing about her new freckles brought out by the sun. Chelsea felt closer to blotchy lobster.

"Not exactly **with** Kai," Chelsea said. "He's a black belt. What I do is more like a workout. The coach shows us all the moves, and we do them to music." Chelsea was still buzzing from her first two classes. She loved the energy they had given her.

"You can do a workout at home, hun. With me," said Lena. "We could look online for a video this afternoon."

"Like we'd really do that regularly," Chelsea said, shaking her head.

"I could come to the gym with you, then," said Lena.

Lena's puppy, Robbie, began chewing her towel. Lena nudged him away. "Who else is in your class?"

Chelsea hesitated. If she told the truth – that it had been two grannies and some junior age kids – she wouldn't look cool. "Just a mix really."

"Any decent guys?"

"Nope," said Chelsea.

"That's me out then." Lena sat up as her phone buzzed. "Kai's texting. He's with Sanjay. They want us to meet them in the park."

Chelsea sat up too. The thought struck her that it was always Lena who Kai texted first. Never her. Sometimes it felt that if she wasn't with Lena, she was invisible.

"Think I'll head home. Tommy's back next weekend and I'm supposed to help Mum paint his room," Chelsea said.

"I'll help," Lena offered. "We'll meet the others later."

"Better if it's just me," replied Chelsea. "Mum gets super-wired when Tommy's due home. She'll probably have endless jobs for me to do."

Chelsea pulled on her shorts and T-shirt over her bikini. The truth was, she didn't really have to help Mum. She wanted to practise the kickboxing moves. She knew it was pathetic, but she wanted to get praised by Liz.

She might turn out to be better than those two grannies and the schoolboys.

"Promise you'll text when you're done? We can come and meet you," said Lena.

"Maybe." Chelsea shrugged. She was still feeling prickly about being the loser no one could be bothered to text. Perhaps Whitney was right. Perhaps she really didn't matter at all.

Out in the street, she pulled her phone from her pocket. Maybe she shouldn't have been so moody.

If she saw that Kai or Sanjay had texted her as well, then she would change her mind and meet up with them.

The screen was blank. No messages.

She wiggled her hand in front of her as she walked, just to check she wasn't really invisible.

Chapter Four
Hotting Up

The following week Chelsea was back at Spitting Tiger. "Jab. Jab. Punch. Hook. Jab," she muttered as she punched at thin air.

"Back again, Chelsea?" Liz stood on the stairs of the basement, smiling. "You know there is no beginners' class today don't you?"

Chelsea felt her face blush. "I came with my friend. He's training upstairs. Darren said it was OK for me to practise down here and…"

"I wasn't about to tell you off," Liz said. "I'm pleased you're getting the bug after just three classes."

Chelsea looked at Liz. "I don't normally do sport, but you make it cool," she said.

Liz smiled again. "I was the same when I started. I got obsessed. I would go home and practise round the house, pretending to punch everything and anyone. I drove my husband mad."

"You were a grown-up when you started?" said Chelsea with surprise. "I thought you must have been doing it forever."

Kai started kickboxing when he was nine, so Chelsea thought it must be too late for her to get anywhere close to his level.

"My husband wanted me to try it because I was hopelessly shy. Sometimes I felt invisible," said Liz.

Chelsea was shocked. Liz used to be shy? "Sometimes I feel that way too," she said.

Liz looked hard at Chelsea. "Tell you what, let's run through some moves. I've got time before my next class."

"You sure?" asked Chelsea.

"More than sure," said Liz.

The next hour was like a dream. Liz got a punch bag, and found some gloves and a helmet. Chelsea worked on her front, side and roundhouse kicks.

Liz said she had an awesome uppercut punch which would really help when she got to tournament level.

"Tournament level? No chance." Chelsea stopped punching and frowned at Liz. Tournaments were definitely a step too far.

"Why not? You're good," said Liz. "Video yourself. You'll be surprised. Look, there's a kickboxing display closing the tournament. I'd like you to represent my beginners. I need to get ready for the next class now, but think about it."

Just then Kai appeared.

"You look the part," he grinned, nodding at the gloves Chelsea was pulling off. "You been OK?"

"You bet," Chelsea grinned back.

She headed out of the gym with Kai. Liz thought she was good. Liz believed in her. She opened her mouth to tell Kai that she might even be in the tournament...

... but Kai spoke first. "Got a secret to tell you," he said. "Darren says I can be fast-tracked to second Dan. That means I'll be a higher grade of black belt. I've got to keep it quiet, but I know it's OK to tell you. He wants me matched with the same grade competitor at the tournament. If I win, I'll get a sponsorship deal from a sportswear company. I'll get publicity. Better fights. I might even make the European Championships."

Chelsea loved it that Kai trusted her with his secret. "That's amazing. Awesome!" she said.

Kai put his arm round Chelsea's shoulder. "Just keep telling me," he laughed. Then he sniffed his own armpit. "Disgusting, sorry. I'm hot and stinky."

"Stinky is good," Chelsea grinned. "It goes with the kit."

Kai laughed again. "Just keep those compliments rolling in," he said.

Chelsea was trying to focus on being normal, but having his arm round her gave her a melting feeling. Would he really start to notice her if she got good at kickboxing?

Suddenly Kai's phone buzzed.

Kai read the message.

"Almost forgot. I arranged to meet someone," he said. "You go on ahead."

Kai held his phone up to show Chelsea a photo.

Chelsea gasped as a girl stared out from Kai's screen. It was Whitney, the tall supermodel type girl who had laughed at her and said she wasn't important.

Chapter Five
Bad Deal

Chelsea couldn't sleep. She got up early and went to the gym. Tommy always said you should let the past go; well that was what she'd do.

She wouldn't think about Kai any more.

She'd do as Tommy said and fight for the future, and that fight was starting with training. Punching, kicking and jabbing would get the image of Kai and Whitney out of her head. She would feel better. Stronger.

A car with the Spitting Tiger logo was parked outside the gym, which meant Darren was in the building.

But when she went in, there was no sign of Darren. There wasn't even anyone training.

She wondered if it would hurt to jab one of the punch bags with her bare fist.

She looked around. Darren's office door was shut.

Clenching her fist, she raised it level with the nearest bag and jabbed lightly. She did it again, but faster. Harder. Soon she was punching different bags, moving through the gym. She got her phone out and set it to video, balancing it on the bag opposite. Then she punched again. She shuffled her feet, the way Liz had taught her, getting ready to kick.

Suddenly, she heard voices.

"It's all sorted, Ace," said one voice.

"Better be," said the other.

It was Darren, and a young guy. He looked about Tommy's age. He had a huge black dog with him.

Chelsea crouched low. Darren had given her permission to use the basement, but not this training area. If he saw her, he might get angry. He might even throw her out of the club.

But Darren sounded almost scared. "I've done what you wanted. I've moved my boy up a level to second Dan."

"I wish it hadn't come to this, but you should never have borrowed money you couldn't pay back," said Ace.

His voice was threatening.

"I thought the new equipment would bring me new members. I got it wrong," said Darren.

"Bad planning. I'll keep my promise – I'll cancel the debt if your kid loses. But, if he beats my top boy then..." Ace looked round at the training equipment, "... I'm afraid I'd have to speak to a couple of my friends. They could pay this place a visit one dark night. Reckon they could empty it in a couple of hours. You remember what happened to the last club that let me down."

"It won't come to that," Darren spoke again. "Kai won't even have the stamina for the full three rounds. He's only trained for fights that last one round."

Chelsea shuddered. She realised that Kai was being set up to lose the fight. Darren had tricked him. She wanted to leap out and punch these cheats, but they would know she had heard every word. Ace might even send his gang of friends after her. She tried to creep away, and edged sideways. Her shoulder knocked one of the punch bags.

The dog growled softly.

The two men were still talking.

"My boy is called Badi Bello and he's going to be world-class. He'll make my club a household name," said Ace.

There was a pause, then he added, "Your Kai will be doing you a favour too. You won't have to close down, just so long as he loses on purpose."

The dog was crouched low, as if it were getting ready to pounce.

Chelsea heard more footsteps. "Morning boys." It was Liz. "Didn't expect to find you here, Ace. Your club is our biggest rival."

"I'm just going," Ace said. "Had some business with Darren."

"See you then," Liz said. "I've got an over-fifties class to teach."

Chelsea watched Ace and the dog leave.

Darren headed back to his office.

Chelsea grabbed her phone, then ran out onto the street.

She texted Lena and Sanjay.

Meet me in the park? URGENT xxx

Between them, they'd decide the best way to tell Kai what was going on.

Chapter Six
Big Fat Lies

"Are you sure you heard right?" Lena asked Chelsea. Lena glanced at Sanjay, who raised his eyebrows and shrugged.

Chelsea saw the look. "You two don't believe me?"

The three of them were sitting on the grass at the park.

Lena threw a tennis ball. Robbie the puppy bounded after it. "We're just a bit worried about you," said Lena.

"Who's we?" Chelsea frowned.

"Me and Lena. Or at least, Lena's been talking to me," said Sanjay, looking uncomfortable. Sanjay was never up for anything awkward.

"You've been a bit weird, since you started kickboxing," said Lena.

"Thanks for that," Chelsea muttered.

Lena touched her arm. "You're moody."

"No I'm not," said Chelsea.

"Well you wouldn't come out last night. I texted loads of times. And last weekend, when we were sunbathing, you left in a bad mood."

Chelsea shrugged. "What's that got to do with everything I've just told you about Kai?"

There was silence.

Robbie dropped the tennis ball on Chelsea's lap and she threw it. It went a long way. She was stronger than she had realised.

"Kai said you looked upset when he told you he was seeing Whitney. Me and Sanjay wondered..." Lena hesitated. "Maybe you're starting to like Kai in a different way. Not just as a friend," she said.

"It's easily done," Sanjay laughed. "Most girls seem to fall for Kai's charms."

Chelsea sprang to her feet. "You think I've made up this story just to get Kai's attention," she said.

"You might want a reason for him to be grateful to you," said Lena gently.

Chelsea's face burned. They were too close to the truth. Some of it, anyway.

"Look, hun, maybe you've muddled things up," said Lena.

"And even if you haven't, how can you prove it? If you tell Kai and he believes you, he will have to challenge Darren. Darren will just cancel the fight. And if you tell Kai and he doesn't believe you…"

Sanjay didn't finish the sentence.

Chelsea looked at them both. Maybe Kai really would think this was just her being jealous.

If Kai thought she was twisted enough to make up such big fat lies, he might not want to know her.

She wouldn't even be a girl **friend** anymore.

Chapter Seven
Genius Genes

Chelsea opened the door of The Crown. Tommy was coming out of the bar. She rushed over to him. "I didn't think you were home until the weekend," she smiled.

"Got out early." Tommy hugged her, then held her at arm's length. "You OK?"

Chelsea suddenly thought about the gym. Kickboxing. Everything that was happening with Kai. Tears came to her eyes.

Tommy looked worried. "Right. You, me and some bags of crisps. We'll sit down and you can tell me everything," he said.

Chelsea sniffed. "It's stupid," she said. "Even my best friends think I'm twisting things round."

"Nothing that upsets my little sister is stupid," said Tommy.

Minutes later, Chelsea let the whole story unfold, in between sipping juice and crunching crisps.

Tommy listened. "I don't think you've twisted anything. And Kai's got to know," he said.

Chelsea was relieved. At least Tommy didn't think she was a jealous liar. But it still didn't mean Kai would thank her. "What if he hates me for telling him?" she asked.

"You've got to risk it," said Tommy. "Being honest doesn't always get you loads of friends, but it gets you the right ones."

"I've got no way to prove anything," said Chelsea. "Sanjay was right. Kai will challenge Darren. The slime ball will wriggle out of it somehow. I know he will."

Tommy looked thoughtful. "Didn't you say you had your phone on video? Recording yourself so you could see how good your moves were?"

"I haven't watched it yet. I'll look rubbish," Chelsea said. Watching her moves had been the last thing on her mind.

"But it won't just have recorded you. It will have filmed those scumbags too," Tommy pointed out.

Chelsea stared at Tommy. "You are a **genius**," she said.

"Well, remember we share the same gene pool," said Tommy. "But you'd better watch the video and check. My genius status could be very short-lived."

Chelsea took her phone out of her pocket and turned it on.

Chapter Eight
Tough Talking

Kai opened the door of his house. "Hi Chelsea. Hey, Tommy. You just get back?" said Kai.

"Yeah," Tommy nodded. "Can we go somewhere private? Just you, me and Chelsea?"

"We can talk here. Everyone's gone out."

Kai led them through to the kitchen. "Something wrong?" he asked. For once, he wasn't smiling.

And he wasn't smiling when he looked at Chelsea's video either. He watched it over and over again. "I've been set up. I'm a mug," Kai said. He slumped at the table, his head in his hands.

"I've got a plan," said Chelsea softly. "It's something Tommy says about being in the army. He says you don't run from the enemy. You deal with them."

Tommy nodded, then said just as softly, "And you, my friend, have got some serious enemies to deal with."

Kai shook his head. "I don't care what they've done. The only fighting I do is in the boxing ring."

"That's not my plan," said Chelsea. "Tommy's super-fit. Even more than you are. He knows how to train every muscle, and he knows all about fighting and self-defence."

Tommy folded his arms. "I'll be your secret coach," he said.

"I'm home for a month and in that time I'll get you up to army fitness. You'll be able to handle anything. You both will."

"Both?" Kai looked puzzled.

"I'm training with you," said Chelsea. "Everyone always says I should stand up for myself more. Being super-fit will do me good. Plus, I might want to join the army one day. Training hard now will help with that too."

Kai looked impressed, but then frowned again. "And then what?" he asked. "If I win, Spitting Tiger will close. I won't be able to carry on kickboxing."

"You won't need Darren if you get sponsored," Chelsea said.

"She's right," said Tommy.

"Besides, we want everyone to see what an awesome kick-boxer you are. I won't be around to watch because I will be back overseas by then, but trust me. This Badi Bello and those bad-boy coaches are going to see what a decent fight **really** looks like."

Chapter Nine
Countdown

Chelsea looked around the tournament. The main ring was in the middle of the hall. Some of the kickboxers were warming up and getting ready for their fights. There were lots of trainers about, and a crowd of people who had come to watch.

Chelsea guessed they were probably friends and relatives of the fighters. She felt a twist in her gut. She was in the display later and she hated the idea of being watched by so many strangers.

She saw Kai walking over to her. Whitney was with him. Chelsea had seen them together around their street a few times, but she'd never had to speak to Whitney before.
"You look awesome in the Spitting Tiger kit," Kai said to Chelsea. "When is your display?"

"Right at the end. It closes the tournament," Chelsea told him.

"I'll come and watch," Kai said.

"Oh, don't." Chelsea shook her head. "I'll be rubbish."

"I don't believe that," Kai smiled. "Liz wouldn't have chosen you if you weren't good enough." He hugged Chelsea.

Chelsea saw Whitney's eyes narrow. She mouthed the word 'rabbit'.

Chelsea thought of something Tommy always said: "face your demons."

Chelsea stood very still, and faced Whitney. It was Whitney who looked away first, turning back to Kai. "Can't wait for your fight, babe," she said. "I want the world to know I'm with a winner."

Darren appeared.

Whitney turned to him. "You OK, Darren? You look stressed," she said, laughing.

Chelsea could tell Whitney liked seeing Darren look stressed. Perhaps she got a buzz when people were unhappy? Chelsea hadn't realised Whitney knew Darren. Kai must have taken her to kickboxing. Her gut gave a little twist, remembering how Kai had introduced her as his girl **friend** that first time. He wouldn't have described Whitney that way.

Darren spoke in a low voice. "Kai, mate. I don't know how to break this to you, but it's not going to happen," he said.

Kai frowned. "What's not going to happen?" he asked.

Darren was sweating. "Can we talk somewhere private?" he asked.

Kai glanced at Chelsea and Whitney, then shook his head. "Nah. Whatever it is, you can tell me here. I don't need your secrets," Kai said.

Darren wiped his hand over his brow. "Your fight. I'm going to cancel it."

"No way," Kai said. "I've trained all summer."

Whitney glared at Darren. "He has to fight. You can't stop it now," she said.

Darren took a deep breath.

"Kai, mate, the guy you're matched with is over there," he said. "I mean, look at him. No way will it be a fair fight."

Chelsea looked to where Darren was pointing. Badi Bello was massive. His hair was shaved with a zigzag pattern. He had a tattoo along one arm. It said 'KILLER'.

"So what?" said Kai. He looked as if he was trying to stand taller. "That does not mean he's the best fighter."

"I – er – look, things have gone wrong," said Darren. "I've done something stupid. Kai mate, I don't want you to fight. We can say you've had an injury."

It was Whitney who spoke next, and her voice spat with fury. "You can't pull him out now. It's all been agreed."

Chelsea was surprised that Whitney was so angry. A bit of her had felt relieved that Darren was giving Kai a way out of a dangerous fight. Did Whitney know the real story?

"Kai, mate, I set you up to lose," said Darren.

"I faked your Dan level. The truth is, I owed Ace money and I agreed he could fix the fight so that you were matched with someone much stronger than you. He wanted his own boy to be sure of winning and getting that sponsorship. I'm sorry."

Chelsea was glad he'd told the truth at last. She still thought he was a slime ball, but at least he hadn't gone through with seeing Kai get beaten up.

Kai looked as if he was about to reply, but Whitney butted in. Her eyes blazed.

"You should have thought of that before you made a deal with my brother," she yelled.

Chelsea looked at Kai. Kai looked at Whitney. "Your brother?" they both said together.

"Whitney's brother is Ace Kershaw," said Darren. "His club is our biggest rival. It's called Kombat-K."

Kai turned to Whitney. "Kombat-K? Badi Bello's club?" asked Kai.

"Yeah. So what?" said Whitney.

"Why didn't you tell me?" asked Kai.

"She must have kept it secret on purpose," said Chelsea.

Whitney glanced at Chelsea, then shrugged.

She turned back to Kai and said, "You got me as your girlfriend. I didn't hear you complaining about that. And I got what I wanted."

"And what was it you wanted?" Chelsea asked. She suddenly felt strong. Like a fighter. "Was it to check up on Kai? Pass information to your brother?"

Whitney stared at Chelsea. It was as if she was seeing her properly for the first time. "My brother is building a world-class reputation with his club," she said.

"You want to build a reputation by cheating?" said Kai. "That doesn't sound like a great thing to me."

"What Ace wants, I want," said Whitney. "He's always looked out for me, and I do the same for him."

Chelsea knew that whatever Tommy did, she'd stand by him too. She didn't agree with what Whitney had done, but she understood it.

Kai looked hurt and angry. "Get lost, Whitney," he said at last.

"You too, Darren. You've both just used me."
He walked off. Chelsea hurried after him. "Kai,
I'm so sorry. Is there anything I can do?"

Badi Bello was flexing his muscles over by
the ring. They rippled when he moved.

"Just cheer for me," said Kai. "I'm more
than up for this."

Chapter Ten
Fight

The bell rang. The crowd cheered.

Chelsea yelled, "Come on Kai!"

"They haven't started yet," laughed Liz, hurrying over and sitting beside her. "I need to film this."

But even as she got her phone ready, Kai jabbed a punch at Badi Bello.

Badi kicked back.

"Jab jab, punch, kick," muttered Chelsea, her eyes following every move.

"Kai's fast," Liz said. "Badi's strong, but Kai's got the speed."

Kai bobbed and weaved, then side-kicked Badi into the corner.

"Go, Kai, go," yelled Chelsea.

Badi twisted away. He struck Kai with his knee. Kai span back with an elbow strike. "Front kick, then punch," shouted Chelsea, suddenly feeling like an expert. "Is Kai winning?" she asked Liz.

"Kai is scoring the most points. He's set the pace," said Liz.

The bell went for the end of the first round. Ace ran forward to give Badi water. Darren did the same for Kai.

Liz nudged Chelsea. "See that man in the suit?" Liz said. "That's the owner of the sportswear company. He is the one offering the sponsorship deal."

The man had dark glasses on. They made it impossible to know what he was thinking. Chelsea crossed her fingers. "Please let Kai win. Please, please," she thought.

The bell rang again.

Kai had made it to round two. But then things changed.

"Badi is attacking now," whispered Liz. "He's changed his strategy."

Kai was against the ropes, his hands up, protecting his face. Badi jabbed and punched.

"Kai's looking tired," said Liz.

"Come on, Kai," screamed Chelsea.

Kai fell against the ropes.

"DOWN. Ten... nine..." The referee started counting.

Kai got up but Badi came at him, knocking him down again.

"DOWN. Ten... nine... eight... seven."

Kai pulled himself back up. Badi jabbed and punched.

Suddenly, there was a shout from the corner. "Don't risk it Kai. You've done enough."

Darren was leaping into the ring, pushing Badi out of the way.

A roar came from the other corner. "You idiot," shouted Ace, as he rushed forward. He jumped at Darren, kicking so high he knocked Darren off balance. Darren kicked back. Ace twisted sideways. Then the two of them fell, wrestling, to the floor.

The crowd were on their feet, shouting and yelling.

The referee tried to pull the two men apart. Everyone seemed upset.

"This is madness," said Liz, standing up. "They're behaving like schoolboys. In fact, worse than schoolboys. None of the boys in our club would act like that!"

"What happens now?" asked Chelsea. She stood up too.

"Both the coaches came into the ring. The tournament rules mean if that happens, both fighters get disqualified," Liz explained.

"That's very harsh. It wasn't their fault," Chelsea said.

"We have to follow tournament rules. I don't suppose anyone ever imagined they would apply to two brawling coaches," said Liz. "The rules are just meant to stop coaches fussing round their competitors once the fight has started. To be fair, it was a good fight until this happened. Kai can feel proud. He didn't lose."

At that moment, the referee yelled, "No contest!" Kai and Badi shrugged, then they saluted each other. Chelsea thought it was good that they respected one other. They were true professionals. Badi wasn't bad at all.

Darren and Ace were arguing with the referee. They looked ready to start fighting again.

Kai stepped out of the ring and Chelsea hurried over to him. "Did you get hurt?" she asked.

"Nah. Just a few bruises," Kai replied. Just then, Darren left the ring too. He hobbled over to Kai.

They stared at each other.

"I just lost it, mate," Darren said. "I'm sorry. Again. But you've really proved yourself."

Kai shrugged. "And you, Darren? What have you proved?" asked Kai.

"I've proved that I'm an idiot. Does that make you feel better?" asked Darren.

Kai hesitated. "You've been a good coach. It hasn't all been bad," Kai said.

For a moment Chelsea thought Darren might actually cry.

"Thanks, mate," he said softly. "That means a lot."

Chelsea looked from one to the other. They both looked sad. "What will happen now?" she asked. "Will Ace still come after you for the money?"

They all turned towards Ace. He was standing with Whitney at the back of the hall. He looked furious.

Darren sighed. "The deal was that Kai wouldn't win. So, you could say I kept my side of the bargain. But Ace will get his money. I haven't told him yet, but I'm selling Spitting Tiger. I'm moving to Spain."

Kai looked gutted. "Spitting Tiger's going to close?" he said.

Liz walked over to them. "I'm taking it over. Darren and I agreed the deal just before your fight." Liz shook her head at Darren.

"You certainly can't come back after that stupid fight with Ace. But I need to talk business with you. There are things I need to check," she said.

"Yeah, sure," said Darren. He turned back to Kai. "Maybe one day I'll be able to do something good for you, mate. Put things right."

Darren and Kai shook hands. "I'd like that," Kai said.

As Liz and Darren walked away, Chelsea turned to Kai, "What happens about that sponsorship?" she asked.

"The sportswear guy's going after one of the top ranked girls. He watched her fight earlier. I'm cool with that. It always felt like a crazy dream anyway," Kai said. Suddenly he looked worried. "Do you think Tommy will think I fought OK?"

"He'll think you were awesome. Liz filmed it, so he'll get to see it," said Chelsea. Things had worked out. Darren was leaving. Ace's club wouldn't get to be a household name. "Just one thing though…" began Chelsea.

"What?" asked Kai.

Chelsea took a deep breath. "What about Whitney? Are you upset?" she asked.

They both looked across at Whitney. Chelsea still thought she looked like a supermodel. Surely Kai must still want to be with her?

He shrugged. "Nah. She's bad news," Kai said.

He put his arm round Chelsea. Chelsea ignored the usual goose bumps. She sniffed loudly. "You've got armpit-stench again. You truly are disgustingly stinky," she laughed.

"That's what's awesome about you. You're always honest." Kai grinned. "Thanks for being my mate."

Chelsea grinned back at him. Tommy was right. Being honest may not always get you loads of friends, but it gets you the right ones.

"Thanks for being my mate, too," Chelsea said.

"Hey, Chelsea..." Liz tapped Chelsea on the shoulder. "Time to warm up. Your kickboxing display is on in just ten minutes time."

"Go for it," said Kai. "I know you'll be awesome."

"I'll do my best," grinned Chelsea. She gave Kai a playful punch on the shoulder. They both laughed. Still grinning, Chelsea walked with Liz to join the rest of her team.

Bonus Bits!

About the Author

Here are some interesting facts about Judy Waite.

- she was born in England but was raised in Singapore
- she has published over 40 works of fiction
- she runs creative writing workshops in schools for pupils *and* teachers
- she works at a university and lectures on creative writing to students

Who's Who?

Match the character with their description:

A Liz

B Kai

C Lena

D Tommy

E Robbie

F Darren

G Whitney

    1 Chelsea's older brother

    2 Head of the kickboxing club

    3 Chelsea's best friend

    4 a bully

    5 Lena's puppy

    6 runs the beginners' kickboxing class

    7 one of Chelsea's friends

Quiz Time!

How well can you remember the story? Try answering the questions below. Look back at the story if you need to. The answers are at the end (no peaking!).

1. What had Chelsea never told Lena?

    A she had fallen out with her brother

    B she had a pet rabbit

    C she had a secret crush on Kai

    D she loved kickboxing

2. What was on the clothing that most people in the gym had on?

    A Hissing snake logo

    B Spitting tiger logo

C Growling tiger logo

D Angry snake logo

3. What secret does Kai tell Chelsea?

A That Lena's puppy is poorly

B That Darren is going to sell the club

C That he fancies her

D That Darren can fast-track him to a higher level of black belt

4. Why do Lena and Sanjay not believe Chelsea?

A she has told lots of lies before

B they never listen to her

C they think she has made it up

D they don't like her

5. Who is Whitney's brother?

   A Sanjay

   B Darren

   C Badi Bello

   D Ace Kershaw

6. What tournament rule has to be followed when both coaches enter the ring?

   A both coaches have to fight

   B both fighters are disqualified

   C both fighters must leave the ring

   D both coaches must leave the building

WHAT NEXT?

If you enjoyed reading this story and haven't already read *Sanjay's Story*, grab yourself a copy and curl up somewhere to read it!

Have a think about these questions after reading this story:

- Do you think Chelsea was right to tell Kai what she had heard?
- Why do you think Whitney was with Kai?
- How did Chelsea's confidence change throughout the story?
- What do you think would have happened if Chelsea had not overheard the conversation?

ANSWERS to WHO'S WHO?

A6, B7, C3, D1, E5, F2, G4

ANSWERS to QUIZ TIME?

1C, 2B, 3D, 4C, 5D, 6B